SESAME STREET

Elmo's Delicious Christmas

D1414609

Written by Michaela Muntean and Elizabeth Clasing · Illustrated by Tom Leigh

Dalmatian Press, LLC, 2005. All rights reserved.
Published by Dalmatian Press, LLC, 2005. The DALMATIAN PRESS name and logo are trademarks of Dalmatian Press, LLC, Franklin, Tennessee 37067. No part of this book may be reproduced or copied in any form without written permission from the copyright owner.

Printed in the U.S.A.
ISBN: 1-40371-579-3 (X) 1-40371-883-0 (M)

06 07 08 LBM 10 9 8 7 6 5 4 3 2
14376 Sesame Street 8x8 Storybook: Elmo's Delicious Christmas

It was the day before Christmas, and Elmo's kitchen smelled like sugar and cinnamon. That was because Elmo was helping his mommy and Aunt Sue bake big batches of Christmas cookies.

Elmo got to make the shapes with cookie-cutters and sprinkle on sugar that was glittery white or in bright Christmas colors.

Elmo's mommy clicked on the oven light so Elmo could watch the cookies turn golden brown. As soon as they came out of the oven, Elmo reached for some.

"Wait until they cool, and then take just one, Elmo," Mommy said. "We have to save the rest for our guests." Elmo nodded but it seemed to take forever!

"*Now* can Elmo pick one?" Elmo asked when the cookies were cool. "And will you tell everyone that Elmo helped make them?"

Mommy said that Elmo could tell them himself. This year he was big enough to hand out the cookies at the family's Christmas party.

Elmo smiled and picked out a cookie shaped like a reindeer.

"Mmmm… yummy!"

As Elmo's mommy tidied the kitchen, she glanced out the window. "Look, Elmo! It's snowing!"

"Oh, boy! Mommy, may Elmo please go outside to play?" Elmo wanted to know.

Mommy said yes, so Aunt Sue helped Elmo with his coat and boots. "And here's a nice, warm scarf to tie around your neck," she said.

Cozy and warm, Elmo ran down Sesame Street to build a snowmonster. He saw footprints his boots made in the new snow—snow as pretty and white as the sugar Elmo had sprinkled on top of the cookies.

Snowflakes drifted down and sparkled on Elmo's hat and scarf. He opened his mouth to catch some on his tongue.

All along Sesame Street, Elmo saw his friends getting ready for the
holidays. Ernie and Bert were carrying a Christmas tree and Big Bird was
decorating. Herry Monster had dressed up like Santa Claus, and he was
collecting toys and food for families who needed help.

Meanwhile, The Count counted snowflakes as they fell. "One beautiful
snowflake! Two beautiful snowflakes! Three, four, five, six, seven, eight…
so many beautiful snowflakes! Wonderful!"

"Merry Christmas, everybody!" Elmo shouted happily.

As Elmo passed by Oscar's trash can, he wished his friend Merry Christmas, too.

"Humph! I hate Christmas!" said the fuzzy, green grouch.

Elmo couldn't believe his ears. "Would you please say that again, Oscar?"

"Of course I will," Oscar grumped. "I'll say it again and again and again. I hate Christmas. There's all that *ho-ho-ho*-ing and *fa-la-la*-ing. Everyone going around smiling and being cheerful and giving each other presents. This is the worst time of year for grouches."

"Oh, Oscar!" Elmo giggled. "There are things about Christmas even a grouch would like."

"Name one," Oscar said.

Elmo thought for a moment. "Christmas cookies! Elmo helped bake some."

"Were they sardine cookies with squishy icing?" Oscar asked hopefully.

Elmo had to admit they weren't. They were oatmeal and sugar cookies. And some were shaped like candy canes and reindeer.

Oscar scowled. "Yucch! They sound awful!"

Elmo forgot all about building snowmonsters. Now, he had something more important to do. "Just wait, Oscar!" Elmo said. "Elmo will be right back! Elmo is going to find a *zillion* reasons for Oscar to like Christmas!"

"Don't worry. I'm not going anywhere!" grumbled Oscar. And he disappeared inside his trash can, slamming down the lid.

Elmo set off. If he couldn't find a zillion reasons, he was sure he could find a few.

First, Elmo stopped at Big Bird's nest. Elmo told him what he wanted to do. Big Bird said, "I've got an idea! Meet me at Oscar's trash can in one hour."

Next, Elmo went to see Bert and Ernie, who were trimming their Christmas tree. They said they'd help, too.

Then Elmo visited The Count and Herry Monster. Everyone agreed to meet at Oscar's trash can.

Elmo raced home and told Aunt Sue there was something special
he wanted to make. This time, *she* was the one who couldn't believe
her ears.

"That sounds disgusting," Aunt Sue said doubtfully. But she helped
Elmo anyway.

When everything was ready, Elmo hurried over to Oscar's. His friends were there, just as they had promised.

"Merry Christmas, Oscar!" Elmo called as he knocked on the trash can lid.

Oscar popped out. "I told you, I hate Christmas!"

Elmo laughed. "Not for long!"

Before Oscar could tell everyone to scram, Ernie and Bert handed him a scraggly little Christmas tree. It was decorated with a grouch in mind, with orange peels and bits of raggedy string.

"Hey, that's not a bad-looking Christmas tree," Oscar admitted.

"See, Oscar," said Elmo. "That's one thing to like about Christmas!"

Big Bird knew something else that could make Oscar change his mind.

"I like Christmas because it's a time for families to get together," said Big Bird.

"So?" Oscar muttered.

"So, maybe Grungetta would come and visit if you invited her," suggested Big Bird. Grungetta was Oscar's best and grouchiest friend.

"Hmmm…." said Oscar. "That's not the worst idea I've ever heard."

Next it was Herry's turn. "I like the holidays because they're about helping others," he said. "Today, I collected toys and food for families who need them. Tonight, Grover and I are going to deliver them. Do you have anything to share, Oscar?"

Oscar frowned. "Just a minute," he said, disappearing into his trash can.

A few seconds later he was back. "Here. Maybe somebody could use this," Oscar said, tossing Herry a brand-new, red-and-white-striped scarf.

"Thanks, Oscar," said Herry. "Doesn't it feel good to help someone else?"

"Well, it sure feels good to get rid of that scarf. It doesn't have one moth hole in it," Oscar said. But Elmo saw him hiding a little smile.

"Oscar, Elmo made twelve reasons for you to like Christmas!" Elmo added happily. "Here are a dozen sardine cookies with squishy icing. Merry Christmas, Oscar!"

"Ah-ah-ah!" The Count laughed. "Now *there* is something else to like about Christmas… your friends! Let me count them for you… one friend… two friends…"

"Never mind, Count! I can do it," Oscar said grouchily.

Oscar was quiet for a minute. Finally he turned to Elmo. "You were right, fuzz face. Christmas isn't so bad after all." He took a bite out of a sardine cookie. "And these cookies are disgustingly delicious. Thanks. And... Merry Christmas!"

Then everybody began to sing. And Oscar sang *fa-la-la* the loudest.